Mina and go to the Clinic

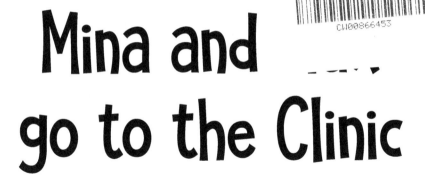

By Delma Venudi-Geary
Art by Jay-R Pagud

Library For All Ltd.

Library For All is an Australian not for profit organisation with a mission to make knowledge accessible to all via an innovative digital library solution. Visit us at libraryforall.org

Mina and Max go to the Clinic

First published 2018
This edition published 2021

Published by Library For All Ltd
Email: info@libraryforall.org
URL: libraryforall.org

This book was previously produced by the Together For Education Partnership supported by the Australian Government through the Papua New Guinea-Australia Partnership.

This edition was made possible by the generous support of the Education Cooperation Program.

Original illustrations by Jay-R Pagud

Mina and Max go to the Clinic
Venudi-Geary, Delma
ISBN: 978-1-922621-21-4
SKU01609

Mina and Max go to the Clinic

2

Mina went with her mum and baby brother Max to the clinic.

"Max is getting an injection for TB today," said Mum.

"What is TB?" asked Mina.

5

6

"TB is a short way of saying Tuberculosis," Mum replied. "TOO – BER – KYOO – LOW – SIS," Mina said, carefully repeating this strange new word.

"What makes TB happen?" asked Mina.

"TB is a very bad sickness that passes through the air from one sick person to another when they spit, cough or sneeze without covering their mouth properly."

"The sick person will get very skinny and weak. They might even die if they are not careful about looking after themselves and finishing all their medicine," said Mum.

"Is that why I have to cover my mouth when I cough?" asked Mina.

"Yes Mina," said Mum.

At the clinic, the nurse took out a very big injection.

"Oh no," thought Mina to herself, but she whispered in little Max's ear. "Don't be scared Max. You'll be okay."

"Good baby," said the nurse with a smile.

Max turned bright red.

"Waaaaaah!" he cried.

Mina cried a little bit for Max too, but she quickly wiped away her tears.

"Now Max cannot get TB, right Mum?" asked Mina after the injection.

Mum held Max and hugged Mina too.

"No Mina, Max cannot get TB now," she said.

You can use these questions to talk about this book with your family, friends and teachers.

What did you learn from this book?

Describe this book in one word.
Funny? Scary? Colourful? Interesting?

How did this book make you feel when you finished reading it?

What was your favourite part of this book?

download our reader app
getlibraryforall.org

About the contributors

Library For All works with authors and illustrators from around the world to develop diverse, relevant, high quality stories for young readers. Visit libraryforall.org for the latest news on writers' workshop events, submission guidelines and other creative opportunities.

Did you enjoy this book?

We have hundreds more expertly curated original stories to choose from.

We work in partnership with authors, educators, cultural advisors, governments and NGOs to bring the joy of reading to children everywhere.

Did you know?

We create global impact in these fields by embracing the United Nations Sustainable Development Goals.

library for all.org

CPSIA information can be obtained
at www.ICGtesting.com
Printed in the USA
BVHW050253100621
609093BV00008B/1101

9 781922 621214